Tales from the Canyons of the Damned

PRESENTED BY USA TODAY BESTSELLING AUTHOR
DANIEL ARTHUR SMITH

Tales from the Canyons of the Damned 32

First Edition

Special thanks to editor Jessica West

ISBN: 978-1-946777-86-7

Cover By Daniel Arthur Smith

Horror Fiction from Holt Smith ltd
Agroland
Tower
Attack of the Kung Fu Mummies

For Susan, Tristan, & Oliver, as all things are.

Superclasico
Gustavo Bondoni

THEIR PROTECTIVE COLORATION kept them safe. Yellow and blue were more powerful than any other talisman in this particular slum, no matter how much it chafed to have to wear the colors of the Boca Juniors club. Well, they could always bathe afterwards.

"Man, and I thought our place smelled," Dario whispered, wrinkling his nose.

"You know what they say about the *bosteros*," Emilio replied, referring to the fans of their hated rivals. But he kept his voice down. Even with the right colors, they were strangers there and therefore objects of scrutiny. Keeping their voices down would give their audience one less thing to analyze.

Of course, most of the eyes that followed their progress belonged to people whose curiosity was had been nearly extinguished by the noxious poverty and aimless drudgery of their daily lives. The great majority of people would forget them as soon as they passed—

grateful that the strangers hadn't brought violence with them.

"I always thought that was just something we said to put them down."

"Everything people say has some truth to it."

The shantytown seemed to go on for miles. Muddy paths wound between shacks built from that combination of corrugated metal and cardboard that immediately told you that you were in one of the poorest sections of the Third World. And Dario was right. It *did* smell.

"Over there," Emilio said, pointing to one of the few concrete structures in the maze: an abandoned control tower that loomed over the shacks beside it and was the only hint that the place they were walking in had once been a railroad yard...before the poor had overrun it. The tracks had been sold for scrap long ago.

Though it looked close at hand, it took them nearly ten minutes to reach the building. There was only one path that led to the door, and it wound in a spiral around the building a few times, meandering this way and that between the shacks before finally reaching the dark entrance which gaped at them. It had once held a double door, but now stood empty.

Dario and Emilio stopped some thirty feet from the door—where the last curve in the path had led them. "We're going to have a hell of a time getting out again," Dario said.

"Not if we do this right. No noise. If there are other people in there, we just walk away."

"They say she works alone. Other people throw off her magic."

"They say a lot of things," Emilio replied. "I don't even believe she has any magic."

"Then why are you even here?"

"Because the rest of you believe it. Because if I didn't come, someone else would be here in my place, and I'd lose the respect of the *barra*."

"How can you not believe? They've won ten games in a row. They're terrible, but they never lose. It has to be magic."

"I don't believe in that stuff. And besides, we haven't played them yet. The Superclasico is in Monumental Stadium this year. They can never win there." It was true. Boca hadn't won the game between Argentina's two most popular sides on River Plate's home field in years.

"Whatever. Just in case, I have my *gualicho* with me," Dario replied.

Emilio grunted. If that ugly thing made of bones and feathers made the man feel safe, he wouldn't talk it down. The last thing he wanted was for his companion to lose his nerve. "Let's go inside."

"I don't like it. Shouldn't there be guards here if she's so important?"

"I already told you. The woman needs to work alone."

The dim interior seemed pitch dark to eyes accustomed to the sunlight. They stood just inside the threshold, waiting for their vision to adjust. When it did, they saw a cavernous square room lit by a single bare bulb in the center.

Seated on the floor right beneath the bulb was a woman with her back to them. There were a number of items arrayed in front of her: papers, photos, sports shirts and what, in the dim light, looked like the carcass of some rodent. To judge by her long, bedraggled blond hair and slim body, she was much younger than Emilio had expected

The woman was jerking violently, twitching like someone having a seizure. At one point, she raised both hands above her head and brought them down among the paraphernalia. Something shattered with a crash and sprayed small parts into the darkness.

Emilio tapped Dario on the shoulder to get his attention and then motioned for him to go to the left of the girl. He pulled out his knife—a commando blade he'd gotten from a guy who'd been in the army—and pointed to his own chest. The message was clear: Emilio himself would take down the woman.

They walked across the room as silently as they could, even though it looked like the woman was in a world of her own and wouldn't have heard them if they'd approached beating drums. Was she actually performing some kind of satanic rite? Did anyone really believe in that stuff, nearly two decades into the twenty-first century?

His heart beat faster and faster as he approached. He'd never killed anyone in cold blood before, and never imagined that his first would be a woman. But there were unwritten rules about what could and couldn't be delegated to underlings within the deeply hierarchal world of the *barras bravas*—Argentina's soccer hooligans.

About four feet away, he took a deep breath and charged forward. Without hesitation, he covered the woman's mouth with one hand to keep her from screaming and drew the razor-sharp blade across her throat in one violent motion with the other. The knife dug deep, briefly caught on something, then slid along. Blood spurted onto his wrist.

Only after the woman stopped struggling did Emilio stop to think. Something felt wrong. It took him a second to realize what it was: the woman's mouth. It was covered with something.

He looked down at the dead body and pulled his hand away. His victim had been soundly gagged with silver tape.

And he recognized her. It was a face that had been on every TV set in the country for nearly three days: a young high-schooler who'd disappeared on her way home earlier in the week. Everyone suspected she'd been kidnapped.

An icy ball formed in his stomach as he studied her. The rags she was wearing had once been a grey school uniform. Her hands were tied together, which explained why she'd been waving them above her arms. Her bare feet were swollen and purple: he suspected that someone had broken the bones to keep her from attempting to stand.

She'd been placed there as bait for a trap he'd fallen right into.

"Dario, let's get out of here now," Emilio said.

Before his companion could respond, bright lights shone into his eyes, blinding him.

"Now!" Emilio yelled and ran for the only thing he could see: the door and the sunlight beyond it.

As he left the building, Emilio turned to look for Dario, but the other man wasn't there. Out in the open, his sudden fear disappeared, and the man who'd faced countless numbers of opposing fans in one brawl after another was back in control.

But the confidence was short-lived.

Behind him, a scream began. It started out as a man's yell, but gradually increased in pitch as the victim was subjected to unbearable pain. Then it turned ragged and finally, just… stopped. He strained his ears to hear more, but there was no more to come.

Dario.

Emilio ran. He took off down the filthy path, turned muddy by the human waste that flowed down its center. His feet struggled to gain purchase with every step, and he had to concentrate on keeping his balance. The dazed inhabitants of the shantytown turned their heads to watch him pass, but he ignored them.

Pursuit was never far behind. He could hear the footsteps of the men behind him, multiple pairs. He had no illusions regarding the possibility of being able to deal with them. He was very much the visiting team here, and the men he would be facing if he faltered were hard men, used to living a criminal life... just like he was.

His breath grew labored.

Where is the exit? The muddy paths seemed to twist into each other, the houses all looked the same—the inhabitants expended no energy in making them different—and offered no landmarks. Still, he knew that if he ran fast enough, and turned often enough, pursuit would falter; in fact, the footsteps behind him seemed to be getting further and further away.

He made another sharp turn and put on a burst of speed. It was a calculated risk: he expended his very last reserves to do it, but knew that his pursuers would never be able to guess which way he'd gone.

Then Emilio stopped suddenly.

Right in front of him was a familiar structure: a concrete tower with a gaping empty door. He knew the door led into a dark room with the body of a murdered girl inside.

"So good of you to come back to us," an old lady said.

This one did look like a witch. Scraggly grey hair framed rheumy eyes, and her smile held more gaps than teeth. She nodded and two men appeared beside Emilio.

He turned to face one, but the other must have hit him in the back of the head with something. Blackness beckoned.

"So, you boys are from the River Plate crowd?" The voice croaked and rattled.

Emilio opened an eye. The pain in his head was almost unbearable, but he struggled to come fully awake. The old woman was seated in front of him.

He tried to move, but his arms were firmly tied behind his back. Likewise, his ankles had been silver-taped to his chair. He could see the tape by craning his neck.

He spat and the spittle landed in a pile of half-congealed blood. The girl's body had been pushed to one side, a gruesome rag doll, but the blood was still pooled where it had fallen, and his chair seemed to be right in the middle of it. There was no sign of Dario.

He tried to talk, but the reply caught in his throat and he gagged. The coughing turned to retching and dry heaves. Nearly a minute passed before he was in control of his body again. The old lady watched him impassively, ugly eyes boring into him. He glared back.

"I suppose you must be. That's good. We can watch the match together. Would you like that?"

He spat at her.

Instead of anger, she merely smiled, stood and patted his arm.

"I'll be back in time for the game," she said, and disappeared behind him.

Emilio looked around the room. There was nothing in it, other than the body of the girl he'd killed and the pool of blood. As the afternoon wore on, the light from the doorway dimmed before finally disappearing completely, leaving him with only the dim yellow light from the bulb for company.

He thought about screaming for help, but remembered the vacant faces of the inhabitants of the slum. They wouldn't get involved, and the police probably hadn't been this deep in the shantytown since the lands were first overrun by the poor. He would gain nothing from yelling but the possibility of another beating. At the very least, if he stayed silent, he wouldn't lose his honor.

A noise behind him made him turn. Two men were wheeling a large TV screen mounted on a table into the room. A small boy behind them had a long extension cable looped around his arm.

The old woman walked over to him.

"You're lucky. You'll get to watch the game today."

He heard another cart rolling up behind him, but when he turned to see what it held, he couldn't spot it.

The men with the TV had finished setting it up. The image was grainy and of low quality, but good enough to see the players warming up on the field of play.

As the national anthem played and the players lined up in the middle of the field, the old woman sat cross-legged on the ground in front of him and, ignoring the dried blood, began to chant, slapping the concrete floor with her hands and swinging her head wildly from left to right. In the light of the bulb and the TV set, the effect was ethereal.

"I don't believe in any of this," he said loud enough for the men in the corners to hear him too. "You're just a fraud."

The old woman ignored him and continued for a few moments more. Then, with a final yell, she stopped and slowly picked herself up. She gave him a wide grin that allowed him an excellent view of the few rotting teeth that remained to her. "The good thing is that you don't need to believe for it to work."

The players were taking their places on the field. The woman walked around him three times then stopped behind him, where he couldn't see, but he heard the sound of metal against metal. They must have rolled some kind of cart loaded with things up to his back. He swallowed, remembering how easy it had been to slit the girl's throat, and wondered if he would soon share her fate. He swallowed and kept his eyes on the screen.

The match had started. If Dario had been in his place, the spectacle of watching River playing the hated Boca team would have been enough to make him forget his predicament; for a couple of hours, he would have forgotten all about the fact that he was tied to a chair. His life's one consuming passion was the River soccer team... and that truly superseded anything else. He fought against the fans of other teams for reasons that might best be described as religious. Not accepting that Rover was the pinnacle of existence was, to Dario, heresy.

Emilio differed. He was a casual soccer fan at best. His concerns had more to do with the power that could be achieved—even from humble beginnings—among the fan organizations. One worked one's violent way up the ladder, from the fringes and dope dealers all the way to the center, literally the center, of the main grandstand, which was where the bosses of the *barra* held sway, the men who received the payoffs to provide muscle to political campaigns and who controlled the drug dealing in vast swathes of the Buenos Aires metropolitan area. As the camera panned over the spectators, he wondered if anyone missed him, or whether some lower-ranked lieutenant was already using his absence to try to get that one step closer to the top.

The woman walked back into his line of sight. She was holding a long, thin knife.

"I'm not afraid of you," he said.

"I don't care about that. Those macho games are things men play among themselves. I'm sure my companions over there are very impressed, but I have other duties." She sliced into his shirt, removing a square of cloth above Emilio's stomach. She spoke while she worked. "I wasn't always a witch, you know. Once, I was a doctor. A thoracic surgeon, to be precise. But they sent me to jail for harvesting organs. They said that my patients would not have died except for my negligence. They said I'd killed them for personal profit."

The old woman spat and turned to watch the game. It was still scoreless, so she sat cross-legged and observed the match in silence.

Not having any other choice, Emilio watched with her.

About twenty minutes into the first half, River scored a goal. He screamed the word *goal* as loudly as he could. He might be the prisoner of the rival faction, but he wouldn't show them that he was afraid, despite the crawling sensation in his stomach.

He expected the big guys to beat him to a pulp, but instead, it was the woman who reacted. "This is too bad," she said, shaking her head sadly.

Getting back to her feet with difficulty, she approached him.

"I never killed a patient in my life, and negligence... I was the best surgeon in Argentina. No one died needlessly on my watch. They were all selling the organs of the dead patients, but they came after me because I was a woman."

She poked a finger into his stomach, and for some reason that single gesture brought all his fear to the fore. It was all he could do to control his bladder.

"I learned to control the spirits in jail. Have you ever been to jail? I don't think so. The *barras* have politicians behind them. You never go to jail, do you? In jail, you need power, and the way I got it was by befriending a witch. She taught me what she knew... and she took her price."

"I don't believe in any of that."

"I already told you. What you believe doesn't matter." Without any expression, she made an incision all the way across his stomach, just above the belly button, from left to right.

Emilio screamed. He screamed until his world was nothing but screams and then he screamed again. Finally, he gathered himself enough to ask: "What are you doing?"

"Nothing you believe in," the witch replied. She gestured to one of the men behind him. Tough hands took him by the hair and wrapped tape around his head several times, covering his mouth comprehensively. "Now you need to be quiet. You wouldn't want me to lose my concentration and kill you by mistake, now would you?"

She started playing with the loose folds of skin and Emilio looked away. Unable to scream, the pain seemed somehow worse. He writhed in the chair. Blood soaked his pants.

When he looked down, the old woman was holding something in her hands that looked like a snake. With horror, he realized that it came from within him: a length of his entrails. This time, he couldn't control his bladder—or anything else.

He must have passed out because her voice in his ear brought him back to consciousness. "The first incantation worked wonderfully," she said. "Opening you up for the spirits has made them receptive to my spell. I asked them to give me something in return, and they did. Look."

The score was one to one.

The woman patted him on the shoulder. "But you don't believe in any of that, of course." She sat by the TV, watching intently. "Let's see how it goes from here."

He felt weak, but somehow managed to stay awake for the halftime interval and the beginning of the second half.

The woman spoke again. "For most spells, animal offal, mainly from chickens, is enough. The spirits aren't greedy. Small attentions suffice." The she turned to the screen showing the most important soccer match in the country, one of the most important anywhere in the world. A game that millionaires from Europe flew in to see, and that was consistently ranked among the top can't-miss sporting events by the world press: Boca-River, the Superclasico. "But some things are too big for that. They demand more."

She watched the game in silence for some minutes. Time was running out, with only ten minutes remaining in the second half.

"Well, I guess it's now or never." The woman returned to him and, pausing only to reach over his shoulder to pick up a plastic bottle of alcohol, began to pull at his entrails, slopping them into a pile at his feet. He screamed into the gag, but there was nothing he could do. Blood spurted in every direction. How was it possible for him to remain conscious? Shouldn't he have lost too much blood?

He felt his consciousness slipping but fought to stay awake.

The witch-woman doused the pile of guts, still connected to his body, with alcohol. He couldn't understand why she was trying to keep him disinfected. Would that save his life? Surely, she couldn't put all of that back in, could she? Whatever the answer was, she emptied the entire bottle onto his entrails.

Then she looked up and, apparently surprised to see that he was conscious, gave him a rotting smile. "It would probably be better for you not to watch this next part." In a single fluid motion, she struck a match and dropped it.

Foomp!

The alcohol caught fire and the smell of cooking meat reached him.

Emilio screamed and screamed. He couldn't feel the pain from his stomach, but his legs were on fire.

A noise from the TV caused him to look up. Yellow-and-blue-clad players were hugging each other in celebration. Boca had scored a goal.

The score was two to one when the referee blew the final whistle. River, the club he loved and to whose hard-core fans Emilio belonged, had lost.

After that, everything went dark.

The Fourth
M. M. De Voe

WHEN LORD ZHYKLON INVITED ME to the head table to play an ancient game with him, I felt blessed. I thought it proved my worth. My father had tutored me intensely in chess and Go and several other old strategy games, and so far in my twenty-six years, this ability had never been of any use except to attract gamer boyfriends. And girlfriends. I'm not that picky when it comes to the bits—I'm more attracted to what's between the ears. Frankly, I was so sick of being seen as a trophy (cute girl who's smart? I win!) that when the summons came—in the form of an enchanted scroll on human skin, of course—I accepted immediately, even though it radiated pure evil. Yes, I knew that no one ever survived a meeting with Lord Zhyklon. Sure, I was vastly uncomfortable with touching the scroll at all, human rights and fair trade and all that stuff you pick up at a liberal arts college, but I figured if I could handle myself with rival lovers on the same panel at a werewolf con in Idaho, I could damned well face whatever foul creature had asked me to burn a black candle and chant its name three times while inverting my eyelids and licking my lips.

No easy task, mind you. I wasn't allowed to use my hands to invert my eyelids. Took a while to get it. But I can also tie a cherry stem with my tongue without cheating, so there's that.

Anyway.

One of my exes—a balding, twice-divorced guy with a neon green Vespa—was avidly into Pathfinder, GURPS, and D&D, so I knew my way around role-play. This likely also explains why I hadn't immediately taken my own life once I realized the spell had worked and I was trapped in an evil alternate reality. I initially regained consciousness in an opulent 18th-century locked bedchamber, holding only my dead cellphone instead of the creepy scroll I'd been chanting from while LiveTweeting the ceremony.

I did not hesitate to toss the now-useless phone onto the brocade bedspread and immediately change into the old-fashioned corset I found set out for me there. I tightened the laces, pulled on the multiple petticoats, the hoop frame, more petticoats, then the yellow satin dress. Believe me, I'd done my share of roleplay for both genders—I knew what was expected. Scrambling over to the mirror, I did my hair in an updo from the 1800s I'd learned for cosplay and placed the curls fetchingly across my forehead. Then I checked once again if there was phone signal (the phone wouldn't even turn on) and also to see if the windows were locked (they were), and set about assessing my situation.

I discovered that I was in a tower on an extremely high floor, and furthermore that, although one of the two windows budged open a sliver, the glass panes were tragically unbreakable. I tried the door and received not only another dose of pure evil, but also a relatively severe electric shock. This caused me to return to the window-seat. Believe me, I needed to sit down.

Was the geography that spread off into the distance within my normal universe but at a different time and place, or was I in another dimension altogether? I had already made value judgments based on the décor: the two tapestries showed a white male knight in glowing armor being snapped in half by giant crab claws, and a screaming girl torn in thirds by competing octopi. *Patriarchal Old Europe*, I thought, and therefore I sat with ankles demurely crossed, the provided yellow slippers on my feet. In the distance there were thick evergreens, half-subsuming snow-capped mountains. No other dwellings were visible, though birds of prey sometimes circled through the clouds. The occasional raven laughed as it wheeled past my tower.

Despite the seemingly Alpine surroundings, this castle or multi-turreted mansion (it was hard to tell from my beautiful prison) appeared to live in the middle of a swamp. I say live because who knows? We've all heard stories of sentient castles eating their inhabitants and so forth, and clearly I wasn't in some remote place in my usual dimension. Not only did my cellphone not work, but gravity seemed slightly lessened since I could easily glide across the floor as befitted a maiden in some 18th century alternate reality. Not that I was actually a maiden by patriarchal European definition, but okay; I was young enough and I was cisgender female. By craning my neck, I could just glimpse brackish water and various shadowy reptilian shapes gliding by. Through the small opening in the window, I could also smell an ocean nearby, though my deep calming breaths were often interrupted by startling wisps of methane and sulfur. Occasionally, too, I heard the nearby barking of frenzied hounds as if just before a feeding, but otherwise the atmosphere was quiet, with just the ravens' mocking cries to break the silence.

Time passed. I was fed after a long interval—the food was plentiful and simple, served in the style of an ancient English hunting manor, meaning that my reluctantly shed tears held more salt than either the gravy or the meat. The tray had been brought in by a serving boy, and I thought I might find an ally in him. He appeared human. His eyes were brown and intelligent. He was too young to have been here long. His blond mustache was wispy as if he had not yet been taught to shave. His hair was in a low ponytail and reached the center of his back. He wore clothing reminiscent of someone's 18th century fantasy of the Orient—gold genie pants and slippers that curled up at the toes, with a purple sash and white, blousy sleeves. The outfit looked a bit stupid and I thought I might be able to win his confidence by joking with him about the garb and décor. But I soon discovered that he was not interested in friendship.

He hovered over me until I had returned every piece of china and cutlery to its proper place on the tray. Having nothing to lose, I tried frankness.

"Think I could hold onto this knife, for defense?" I asked.

He wasn't willing to collude.

And he had sharp observation skills. After I finished the watery custard provided for dessert, my wrist was held in a superhuman grip as he twisted the demitasse spoon free and replaced it gently on the tray.

I begged the servant boy not to tell his master what I had done, promised I would help him escape in return, but he only gave me a half-hearted grin in reply. And there I saw my error.

An oily, dark, greenish liquid seeped through his bared teeth, and I moved swiftly back to my window seat in an attempt to hide my disgust and, frankly, fear. He wasn't human. Or at least he wasn't human like I was. I was left alone for twelve hours, wherein I discovered there were no secret panels in the walls, no trapdoors under the elaborate rugs, and not one of the books in the large bookcase opened to a secret escape route. Additionally, the books were all in languages I couldn't read. I was initially happy just to see that books existed in this world, but I soon discovered that it was torture to run my fingers over shelves of accessible knowledge that I couldn't extract.

Not one of the books had pictures.

So, back to the window with me.

There was only one moon, bright enough to erase any constellations that could have helped me know where I was located. Without that app on my phone as reference, however, astrology wouldn't have helped. I doubted this world had the Big Dipper or Orion. Even if it did, what would that tell me? I could no sooner find a physical way out of this castle than teleport.

When being held captive in a patriarchal alternate universe, it's never a good idea to show fear. Even when your wrists and ankles are shackled and you're being led down a long stone staircase to a rank dungeon where the clammy air has not moved for centuries. Even when you see that your cellmate is roped to the wall, his torso torn open, innards dripping down to his feet. You do not complain of the stench. You do not quake. You press your tongue to the roof of your mouth the way you learned in acting class, to activate your eyes while breathing through your nose, leaving your lips relaxed. You don't show your true emotions. Even when you're left there, in the darkness, in your ridiculous yellow gown, without a word. You maintain the role. It seems like you have no other choice—though you recognize that you always have a choice. Acting this way prolongs your life and you very much value your life.

You do wonder, however, at your own gullible nature. I had responded to a request to play a game with someone calling himself Lord Zhyklon. It had never occurred to me that this most basic premise might be a lie. I hadn't considered that the invitation itself might be a trick. I'd only recognized that the person doing the inviting was obviously evil. I'd considered the possibility of abduction, torture, and imprisonment, once the game had been played, but not of the simple lie that there might not even be a game.

Thus, when, many months later, a beast filled the doorway of my subterranean cell—a beast I could smell before seeing, a beast that undulated and swarmed, that blinded me with a fear so great I was sure my head was splitting open—to welcome me to his castle and invite me to be the fourth at a game he was playing upstairs, I was relieved rather than horrified. It made me feel briefly delighted that it hadn't been a trick after all.

I get that this is stupid, but still and all.

I was briefly delighted.

I was.

I fell immediately back into the role-playing nature I had abandoned after months in this dank cell, and knew instinctively that the proper thing to do when confronted by a patriarchal creature from a literal Hell, was not to scream in terror, but to curtsey as low as possible, forehead touching the filthy flagstones, and kindly accept with an *as you please, m'lord,* keeping my eyes lowered. Because first-off, anyone whose father was a Lovecraftian literary scholar in a third-rate community college knows never to look into any god's eyes, and secondly, no one is ever polite anymore, and a polite young person might just get ahead in the world. You never know.

Also, it is easier to breathe near the floor.

Anyway, and I'm ashamed to admit this, it was kind of...well...flattering. It was obvious that few mortals were ever allowed to play with him and even fewer humans. And when you add that I'm a female specimen and this was a Chthulu-esque world, well, it suddenly seemed to me, let's say, a kind of weird honor that he chose me of all the meat puppets in the multiverse. He turned, clearly expecting me to follow, moving fast for someone with no legs. I hiked up my filthy skirts as best I could and ran after him. The steps were slippery, but the thick slime trail he left made it easy to see where to go. My worn yellow slippers were greenish by the time I reached the top. Forty-seven steps up from the dungeons, twenty-six across the flagstone landing, another thirty to the subterranean ballroom where he held game night.

My wet feet were cold—the stone floors seemed to radiate right through the lousy slippers—but I'm certain the pallor this gave my skin would be pleasing to the dank lord. I thought maybe Hastur the Unspeakable or one of the other Great Old Ones would be playing, but no, the room held only a couple of Swedish minions. Could be that the original fourth had been eaten, or killed, or died of fright, or possibly madness took him. But I'm going with Hastur blowing off the invitation. No one seems to honor RSVPs anymore, even in interdimensional pocket universes, even for something as intimate as game night. And according to my dad's endless ramblings, Chthulu's half-brother Hastur is notorious for being irritating for no reason. It seems to me that not showing up to a four-person gaming session is just his kind of thing. Funny, I used to roll my eyes when dad would start on some Lovecraftian gabbling in the car or at dinner, and out of love or dismay, he often stopped the lecture.

How I wished now that I had listened!

I missed my dad with a squeezing, empty pain. He probably would have enjoyed this whole thing despite the "you are going to inevitably die or go mad" ending. He used to say that a person can set his mind to enjoy just about anything.

I decided to try.

Climbing up to the dais where the three beings sat at an enormous wooden table with spiral legs, I avoided the pools of seawater and greenish-gray slime as best I could. The stench was unspeakable, but no worse than I was used to in the dungeons. The familiar servant boy unshackled my wrists, which allowed me to properly curtsey to the minions. I took some pleasure in knowing that I was role-playing exactly as they expected.

I looked forward to beating them at whatever game they were playing.

The two Swedes bobbed their oversized heads. The six eyes on either side of their carpish heads rolled independently of each other. Their lips gaped and closed to the ceiling, and the female seemed to be trying to blow spit bubbles that kept popping. I wasn't sure if this was a sign of respect or disgust, so I repeated my curtsey to each of the Deep Ones in turn, not wanting to offend. The female of the pair ruffled her back spikes. The male waved a twelve-pointed fin. I drew a relieved breath. The air tasted like cold herring.

I've never liked cold herring. Never liked seafood of any kind, truth be told.

"I'm eager to start the game, m'Lord," I said.

The fishy people stared at me.

Lord Zhyklon finally waved a tentacle as if to beckon me to the table, and I took my place in the last of the tall, straight-backed velvet chairs. Zhyklon did not stand for a lady. It made my head ache to think about how his smooth, dripping skin stood at all, or how the impossible shape I had seen in the dungeon had contorted itself into a human chair. Throne, really, with swirling ebony pinnacles that blended with the garden of foggy tentacles sprouting from the ancient one's head. I lowered my eyes to the game board and placed my hands flat upon the table as seemed proper.

Keep your hands where we can see 'em, and all that.

European Rampage was a game I had never played, and I hoped the rules wouldn't be too complicated. The board was simply a detailed map of Europe crafted of wrought iron with gold filigree. There were no borders indicated, although London, Frankfurt, Vienna, Minsk, St. Petersburg, and other familiar cities were marked with large rubies. The smaller cities—Copenhagen, Oslo, Zagreb, Dublin—were marked with emeralds. There were scattered sapphires as well, and I wished I had a working smartphone so that I could identify them.

The servant boy, having shackled my ankles to my chair, stood in a contorted position on a cushion made of the pale tanned skins of some unknown creature. I was reminded of the Venus de Milo, though this boy's hands were intact. In them, he held a thick scroll, which unwound as he read the rules to the game. His voice was a soporific monotone, a torture I had not anticipated, and one that grated more than the shackles, which had a vague S/M titillating aspect.

On and on he droned while green ooze trickled over his chin and down his neck.

While he was reading these endless rules, a snake-man appeared tableside, counted out gold and silver coins, and placed the stacks at my right hand. I'm embarrassed to admit this, but I grew excited. It looked like real money. I touched it. It was. I don't know how a person can tell when foreign money is real, but perhaps it's an innate human trait. I knew without doubt that this money was real. Fifty gold and thirty silver coins: a fortune to a girl who had grown up the daughter of a non-tenured academic. What was I thinking? That I would win the game and go home wealthy? I will tell you that at this point, I suddenly stopped being afraid and looked for the positive side of my predicament. Yes, I was about to join a horribly boring-sounding game with three creatures that seemingly did not speak. But friends: the corn chips in the crystal bowls had not been bought on sale at a Costco. They were probably organic. From non-GMO corn. Artisanal corn chips, individually hand-crafted and fried in some exotic healthful oil.

If there was such a thing.

And this snack had been laid out on this crazy table for whom?

For me, that's whom.

I was the whom.

Not the girlfriend. The gamer.

Me.

And I was damned near unbeatable at board games.

A deep rumbling, like an ocean vortex engulfing a ship with all its doomed sailors screaming, emitted from the ancient being at the head of the table. The sound snapped my attention back to the accounting of the various intricacies of game strategies possible within the complicated rule set, even as a blinding light behind my eyes caused me to wince in pain. I had forgotten that Lord Zhyklon was likely to be able to read minds.

More than an hour I sat, spine erect, fighting the competing stenches of rotting moss and corn chips, palms pressing hard on the table in the hopes that it would keep my eyelids open, as the servant droned the rules. The game was extremely complicated: one had to purchase lengths of pipe to allow liquid to travel from metropolis to metropolis, and the labor to build these pipes cost more when crossing rivers, mountains, or boundaries of populated locations. There were various event cards including avalanches, floods, intentional explosions, dissatisfied work forces, mass starvations, opioid drug use, hailstorms, taxes.... I already hated this game with a passion. Why could the king of madness not have chosen something light and fast like Sushi Go or Exploding Kittens?

I could only hope to play better than his minions without actually beating him. I needed to earn his respect and perhaps he would release me, though hopefully not impregnated or insane. When the reading of the rules finally ended, I briefly released my palms and found them whiter than a vampire's victim from the pressure I had needed to exert to stay awake.

The game began.

Lord Zhyklon, of course, went first. He thought for a long time, debating where to lay his first pipes. Waving tentacles obscured the ceiling, shuffling and twitching as he sorted through various possibilities. The Swedes went next, each also debating several moves before placing their first length of pipe. I was sure that more than an hour had passed before my turn.

This was a torture worse than flaying. If every turn went this way, I would age faster than the game could end.

Six hours later, I was certain of my doom. I had laid a pipe to Gdansk and discovered that I didn't have enough silver to even bribe another player on the cheap, which was in itself an unreliable strategy. In gameplay, I was stuck, incapable of earning, incapable of winning. There was no way out. No safety clause. No release. I was in eternal torment, which the other three players either failed to notice or failed to find important. It then occurred to me that as their fourth, I had made it possible for them to end their game, otherwise it would continue indefinitely. They were immortals. I was not. At some point I would die and in doing so, I would forfeit and their game would come to a satisfying conclusion. They would tally up the money they had earned and declare a winner. All was contingent on me, my constitution. As the only mortal player, I was brought food at intervals, and was allowed the usual breaks for evacuations and to go to the samovar to refill my glass. The tea had properties that kept me alert; by now, days had gone by without sleep.

I could not win, I could not lose. I could not complain. I could only exist another day. And then another.

This was actually living hell.

The worst was the silence. The Swedes jostled each other when their turns ended. Lord Zhyklon himself allowed the servant boy to play his pieces so that he would not slime the board. But I? I was required to play my own turn.

All the chance had left this game long ago. Zhyklon and his minions were amassing wealth at a snail's pace. My presence was irrelevant. I was only the fourth at the table, the timer, the dummy. I moved along the pipes, back and forth, back and forth, between Gdansk and Lisbon, sometimes stopping in Milan. Back and forth, back and forth. I regretted breaking up with each of my exes, particularly the clever computer guy who wasn't particularly good looking but oh how funny he was. I longed for the endless hours of D&D where my elven mage's unconscious body was hidden away safely, awaiting a resurrection spell while I ate Cheetos and watched my forty-year-old boyfriend's ranger fight the Drow. At least in that game, there had been a goal. At least there, the players talked.

The corset bit into my waist and hips. My feet had blistered inside my wet slippers, which would clearly never dry in this dank room. I kept my swollen, aching mind on the game, though tears welled up whenever my turn came. My hands had picked up a tremor and shook as I moved the piece its limited nine lengths. Releasing the token, I gasped for air, certain that I was starting to look more and more like one of the immortal Deep Ones. This game would never end. I could quit and be killed, I supposed, but the one time I allowed myself to think it, one of Zhyklon's many eyes darted my way and narrowed—and I knew that I wanted to live as long as possible.

I could only play. It was my turn again, and again I moved nine paces toward a city that I could not affect. I swayed in my chair, my mind unraveling. I could not win, I could not lose, I could only play. Madness, then. My father had said that stories set in this world always ended in madness or death.

But I wanted agency. If I was going to die or go mad, it would be by my own hand, not some unspeakable god's bizarre will.

It was Zhyklon's turn again. I turned to the Swede closer to me and blew her a kiss.

"Hey. When this game is over, you want to play double solitaire up in my room?"

The other Swede gasped for air and his body slid off the chair. One of his tiny finlike hands clutched at the edge of the game board, and caught. The map tipped towards the Deep One and all the many, many carefully laid pipes and piles of gold and silver avalanched to the floor, splashing in the seawater puddles, rolling across the ornate rug, sticking to the slime. Lord Zhyklon towered over the offender, his skin rippling into a ghastly red that reminded me of the blood on the pelt of a flayed rabbit. His anger was a palpable yellow gas that emerged from pores in his skin. It smelled of dead things and I could see the eyes of the Swede on the floor widen as death took him.

Unfortunately, the emissions continued, unabated, as Lord Zhyklon shrieked and tore the Swede into strips of white flesh and let them fall to the floor. The female Swede died second, gasping like a goldfish. Lord Zhyklon, intent on disemboweling her mate, ignored her.

Evil swept the room.

As the darkness closed in around me, I slipped into a satisfied unconscious swoon. No one ever survived a meeting with Lord Zhyklon, I had known that when I accepted the challenge. I would be killed along with the Deep Ones—there was no question, had never been any question—but I would die smiling. And I wouldn't have to play another minute of that horribly boring and pointless game. And that meant that, in a way, I had won.

Killer Shot

Ann Stolinsky

BARS HAVE A REPUTATION for being noisy. McRyan's fits that stereotype.

Big, burly men sat at one end of the bar, chugging their beers. Boys who wanted to be men sat at the other end, their butts barely covering the bar stools, nursing their lite beers. And, interspersed in each group, the women.

Some beauties sat with each group, laughing and batting their eyelashes. Boys and men alike grabbed their wallets and bought them drinks, hoping to take one of the women home with them.

And then there are the women who were not spectacular beauties, buying their own drinks.

I won't say which group was the happiest, nor into which I fit.

Dim lighting couldn't permeate the smoke-filled interior, wisps snaking their way into each patron's lungs. The pool table stood prominently under a fluorescent light fixture. The sound of the off-key live band masked the click of a cue stick hitting the billiard balls.

My eyes were drawn, as they always were, to the dart board hanging on the south wall. Pinholes in the panels surrounding the target highlighted patrons' blissful misjudgments. I smiled. I had been one of those patrons who missed the mark but a few months ago. No longer.

I ignored the distractions surrounding me, dart in my right hand, its tail between my thumb and forefinger. Not too tight, not too loose. Just right, like Baby Bear's porridge in the Goldilocks story.

My hand dropped to my side as a fool wandered directly into my line of sight. His ambling didn't disturb me. Once he was past, I focused again on the dart board, on the black circle in the middle, bringing my hand back and forth slightly, almost imperceptibly, tuning out the ambiance once more.

The bullseye almost didn't exist—others' lucky shots had occasionally punctured it. I chipped away at the rest of the bullseye. The experience of practicing taught me a lot in the last few months—how to wait patiently for the right moment to attack, how to focus on my target as if it, and only it, existed in the room.

I aimed and let the dart soar. Another bullseye.

"Are you ready?"

I inhaled deeply, smoothed down my skirt, and exhaled.

"Yes, I am."

I stepped back as my lawyer opened the double doors toward me. After he affixed them on each side, he joined me. We walked in together, my head high, eyes focused on the empty bench before me. We strode to the victim's table and sat. The courtroom was filled with the best and worst of humanity. Worst of all was the defendant.

The bailiff entered from a door in the front of the room.

"All rise."

My eyes followed the man in the robes as he ambled from his chambers to the bench. He sat; so did we.

"Miss Stone, are you ready?"

My lawyer turned to me, his hand steady on my chair as I pushed it back. His eyes met mine. He stood when I did. We turned to the judge simultaneously.

"I am, Your Honor."

"The jury has declared the defendant guilty on all counts. The court has heard your victim's statement and agrees with your lawyer that you have the right to decide the defendant's fate."

I nodded.

"While the sentence rendered by the jury is death, the law provides for alternate methods of delivering the sentence when the conviction is for violent crimes against minors. While you are no longer a minor, the despicable actions by the defendant were perpetrated upon you when you were. The law clearly states that when a victim has reached maturity, that victim is allowed to determine the fate of the convicted. If you were still a minor, your mother would be tasked with this choice. In this case, Miss Stone, the court will abide by your decision. You will determine whether the criminal is to die by your hand, giving the convicted a possibility of life in prison instead, or if death is to come quickly by the actions of the court."

I smiled. I knew which choice was preferable.

"Death, Your Honor. By my hand."

"You do realize your choice affords him the chance to survive, to live out his last days in prison."

"Yes, Your Honor. I know."

He was handcuffed, his legs chained together. He fidgeted on the seat, set in the middle of a vinyl pool. Six-foot round, sides three-foot high. A pool out of place in this setting, a pool that should have been found in a backyard with children splashing in it, or at a carnival with a bell attached rather than a black mylar balloon.

The pool stood in a room separated from the audience by glass. Everyone present would be able to see the events as they happened.

The judge called my name. My lawyer walked with me over to the bailiff.

"Are you sure this is what you want to do? If you miss, he gets life in prison instead of the justice he deserves."

"I'm sure. And I won't miss."

The bailiff ushered me through the door to another room, enclosed by glass, except for one, four-foot-wide and six-foot-high empty space where a pane had been removed. *This is sufficient for me.*

The bailiff handed me a dart. One solitary dart. One instrument of death, or renewal of life if I missed. I held it for a few seconds, getting the feel of it, assessing the weight. I looked the bastard straight in the eyes—fear showed in his, but I knew there was strength in mine.

"You can't do it," he sneered. "You know you can't."

My training at the bar paid off. I ignored the distractions, the whispers from the gallery, his alternating pleas and taunts.

"You liked it," his voice rose as his face reddened. "You were a willing participant. You walked around the house with your skimpy shorts and your boobs hanging out of your tank tops. You brought teenage boyfriends home and I saw how they touched your ass." He tried sitting forward, struggled to be released from his bonds.

My calm infuriated and humiliated him.

"You asked for it, you whore!"

He began to shake, his anger and fear producing a physical reaction.

"You can't do this—you *love* me. I was more of a father than the bastard who spawned you!

"FUCK YOU!" he screamed.

I drew my hand back and forth several times as he ranted, aiming the dart. It left my hand as he spoke his last word, its tip elegant in flight. Silence. Then one explosive sound—the pop of the balloon as the dart found its target. His sneer turned to shock, his mouth agape. A lever on the seat, held up only by the balloon, was released. Liquid rained down from the balloon, water bubbling as the two compounds mixed together. The seat tilted forward. Sliding down, his shackled feet bicycled furiously, trying to gain purchase. In seconds, his feet stopped moving as the acid touched his clothing and his skin. It took several seconds for him to be totally submerged, and a few minutes for the acid to finish the job.

The bailiff opened the door to the little room, encouraging me to depart. I looked back at the pool and smiled.

"No, you're fucked."

I walked to the exit without a backward glance.

McRyan's was crowded that night. I was elated that my trauma was over, and I could begin to heal. I wouldn't have to look over my shoulder all the time, wondering, worrying, if he was behind me. I smiled. I could begin to live.

The dart hit the bullseye once again.

A guy I didn't recognize walked toward me.

"Betcha five bucks you can't get another bullseye."

I glanced at him, then let the dart fly.

"Hey, good shot!"

"Thanks." I smiled as I reached for his money. "It's my killer shot."

Hide and Seek

Daniel Arthur Smith

WHEN YOU CHOOSE TO LIVE your life interstellar, run-ins with an acquaintance from one's formative years become rare to nonexistent. Hansen is such an old friend, which is to say that we've known each other since we were small children, attended public preparatory together, and even shared the first years of junior college. So when a hand delivered message arrived to inform me that he was planet-side, I didn't hesitate to accept the invitation to visit him in his penthouse suite.

His penthouse, I should mention, was at the top of the Lassiter Grand, a five-star luxury hotel, which is itself within the pinnacle fifty floors of Providence Six's newest chromium luxury tower, The Chamreal. I'd be lying if I refused to admit that the location alone made the invitation all the more enticing. Please don't think me shallow; it wasn't the luxury suite that drew my keen interest, rather *how* it was that Hansen came to be a resident. You see, he was from a fine family, no questioning that, but not one of vast means, so I knew that whatever circumstances had brought him to his new station would be intriguing to say the least. So it was that the following night found me in the turbo-lift of the Lassiter Grand with a bottle of the best Providence Six had to offer in hand, ascending to her upmost floor.

Already, I was dazzled with the style and taste of the hotel, from the mammoth palm fronds throughout the atrium lobby to the darkened wood trim and intricately detailed red velvet paneling of the lift—all an homage to a simpler, colonial time. Even the rapid ascension of the transit was an elegant experience, lacking any sensation of motion; it was as if the cabin I'd stepped into remained in place while the world outside completely transformed. One moment, I was gazing upon that vast reflective marble floor of the jungle lobby; and the next, the scarlet carpet of the penthouse's cherry paneled anteroom—and the kind face of a beautiful young woman.

By the cerulean iridescence of her eyes, I assumed she was synthetic. Not that the neural lace that generates such a glow is exclusive to syns—out here it's quite common among mortals. I bear the blue glint myself. But from her manner and because she had donned the exquisitely tailored black coat and trousers of a butler, I presumed she was staff.

She greeted me with a bow of her head.

"Good evening, Mister Monroe," she said. "The master is waiting in the library."

"Excellent," I said, offering her the bottle. She took it in hand then, without waiting for me to say a word further, did an about face and proceeded to lead the way down the adjacent corridor. This hall was a wood paneled gallery in the same style as the lift and anteroom but decorated with oils of Earthen floral landscapes, their small ornately gilded frames accentuated by candle-bright amber sconces intermittently spaced between them. It was an interior meant to impress, and succeeded in doing so, but it was when I entered the master parlor that my jaw near fell agape, and not due to the books shelved floor to high ceiling along the side wall or the wide hearth of the working gas fireplace. No—though they too were indeed impressive. I was taken by the transparent outer wall, and beyond, the spectacular fuchsia nebula painting the Providence Six skyline.

Slowly, I moved forward, in awe of the gaseous wonder, and though I'd seen the ghost cloud of the nebula on few occasions before, nowhere near the surface was it presented as beautifully as it was framed here in this room.

"It's no mystery they call it *Eye of God*," said a matter of fact voice from the side of the room.

With a mix of surprise and embarrassment, I spun to see the owner of the proclamation. "Hansen," I said with as due exuberance as I could muster, "as I live and breathe."

"And you, Conrad, look at you," he said, approaching with arms extended. "You haven't changed a day."

Because we had both received our age mods some eighty years back at the fashionable age of twenty-two, it would have been quaint for me to mention that he hadn't changed either; it's rather stating the obvious, and he'd already spent the pleasantry. But embrace we did, as those set apart in this life tend to do on reunion, then rather than spend my compliment on him, I commented on the vista beyond. "I must tell you," I said, "the view from your parlor is exquisite."

"It's quite a location you've found yourself," he said, leading me closer to the transparent wall. "You have the contrast from the ancient," he dropped his gaze from the nebula to the neon laced darkness of the deep canyoned cityscape below, "to the modern."

Indeed, it was a contrast. The structures of the colony surrounding the super luxury towers were a hundred stories above the surface and burrowed yet another hundred or so more below, deep into the subterranean foundation of the original settlement, never touched by more than the light of a neon sky.

And there, gently floating thirty or so meters beneath, as if to punctuate our perch among the highest of the high, was a huge dirigible advertisement, her side brightly lit with an animated holo of the company's consoling geisha fairy—which reminded me. "Oh. Before I forget," I said. "I've brought some of the local elixir for you to enjoy during your visit."

His valet, still standing sentry at the door, stepped forward to present the label.

"*Providence Six, Elixir of Absinthe*," he read aloud. "To see through the *Eye of God*."

"Yes," I said. "So it proclaims. At any rate, highly enjoyable."

"I've heard that the recipe delivers an authentic sensation."

"You've heard correct. The recipe utilizes a synthetic form of wormwood, the key being that the thujone levels succeed in maintaining the *authentic* quality of the experience without the toxicity."

"And you prepare it in the fashion?"

"Exclusively."

"Brilliant. This aperitif will pair excellently with the planned entertainment. Alena, can you please make the preparations?"

Alena bowed her head and exited the parlor, leaving Hansen and I to resume our observation of the nebula beyond.

"Entertainment?" I asked. "What do you have in mind?"

"Something light. An accouterment of the hotel."

"Oh?"

"In a moment," he said. "First, you must tell me about the colonial life. What's it like out here on the perimeter?"

"I'm sorry to report that it's not far different than life back in the Homeland. I'm realizing at this moment I'm spending way too much time Mid-Hi, and not enough in the Upper."

"I'm sure," he said. "But the day to day is all consuming for the lot of us. Is it not?"

"Cheers. Yes. Well. As you sent your messenger, you must know that I'm a company man. My offices are fine, better than some. We do a fair amount of work with the Bureau, maintain the contracts with the mining consortium, the primary industry out here." I shrugged. "But, for the most part, it's mundane. Wine, women, and song, and all that."

"Cheers to wine, women, and song."

"Ha. Indeed. Life has been good but, as I age, there's a challenge to find vigor. I can't say I've embraced mediocrity, but then again, mediocrity has become redefined."

"How so?" he asked.

"I strive for, no, I have a thirst for excellence, even in my day to day."

"So, choosing not to settle. That's the key?"

"No small thing," I said. "If one wants to maintain the façade of enjoyment of life." It was when the words left my mouth that I realized the uncharacteristic candor with which I spoke. "Listen to me," I said apologetically. "Going dark when I should be elated to see an old friend such as yourself."

"But what are old friends without the spice of truth?" he kindly asked. "New topic. I see that we both have the cerulean tint in our eyes," he said, "from the neural lace."

"Yes," I answered. "I had mine implanted a few years back for a business trip far off-world."

"And just how far did you beam?"

"Farther than this mortal shell could easily travel. It's such a routine now. Popping out of one's shell and into another far and away. So much time saved. But you know this. You have your own."

"I do. Yes. Mine was implanted more recently, for the same reason—a trip to the Askar system."

"To the Askar. How fascinating," I said. "Which leads me to ask, how are *you* spending your time these days?"

For a brief moment I noticed that, though the features of his face had remained unchanged, there was a nuance, a confidence if you will, that had been absent in our youth.

"What you mean to ask," he said, "is how is it that I attained the status to warrant a stay in the master suite of the Lassiter Grand?"

"Excuse me for sounding so crass," I said, embarrassed he'd taken my query in such a way. "I didn't mean anything of the sort. I merely meant the same as your inquiry. You know? It's been decades since we've last—"

"It's all right," he said. The side of his mouth curled to a sly grin. "I'm having a laugh. Though, that is the question I want you to ask. It may be boorish, but unabashedly, the one I'd be asking. After all, of all of our year, I wouldn't have called me out as one to elevate beyond my station, to become an Arcadian."

"Now you're being harsh," I said, but the feat was indeed a curiosity, and one I myself had yet to achieve.

"No really," he said. "Martin maybe, Joston, who did in fact became an Arcadian. But me? Miles Hansen? Truth is, I have Melker to thank."

"Melker?" I said incredulously. "Benny Melker? I thought he hated you. I thought he hated everybody. He was always so...dreadful."

"Indeed. But it was his bullying, his constant reminder that I was lowborn—"

"Oh, come now."

"I know, I know. Of course, I was not—if anything, we were peers and in retrospect his family's holdings were scarcely different than my own. But all the same, it was his constant chastisement that drove me to succeed."

"I do apologize," I said. "It was all so long ago. Of course, I remember how inappropriately Benny behaved, but I never realized it would affect any one of us in any peculiar way. I always found him to be rather a gnat."

"A gnat?"

"Yes. A gnat. He'd come buzzing around, and we'd run the other way."

"Ironic. That's precisely my memory," he said. "Remember, and I'm going way back, but remember that game of Hide and Seek we used to play in the yards."

"Oh my. That is way back. We were, what, in our second, third year?"

"I suppose, but what I remember is Melker, running, red-faced. He hated that game."

"Yes," I said. "Fair enough. As I remember, he was inevitably *It*. We'd hide, he'd fight the devil finding us, and then could never keep up in the chase. No wonder he was such a tyrant. I wonder what ever happened to him."

"I dare say that I no longer care."

Hansen may have said he didn't care, but his stiff tone was contrary to the words and left me awkwardly stifled. Fortunately, it was at that moment Alena entered the parlor, wheeling the bar cart. She pushed it over near the fire, between two high backed, brown leather chairs. With a nod, Hansen gestured that we to should move to the fire. "Please," he said. "Have a seat." I circled the cart to sit in the interior chair then he relaxed into the other. As with the wood paneling, I couldn't tell if the leather was natural or synthetic, but it certainly had the scent and soft feel of the former.

Hansen sank back into his chair, but didn't appear to be at all comfortable. "Not quite right," he said.

"And what's that?" I asked.

"The fire," he said, then added, "Landon? Could you turn up the fire a smidge?"

With that, the flames increased in measure.

I inquired. "Landon is the—"

"The house butler," said Hansen. "It's better now. A bit cozier."

I'd never thought of my apartment's digital assistant as anything more than just that. A house AI with the ability to set your schedule or adjust the lights, temperature, and appliances didn't rank anywhere near a butler in my mind—Alena, on the other hand... To have a valet such as her in his service, that was no small matter. At any rate, he was right that it was cozier with the fire turned up. The light of the flames, subdued beneath the mantle a moment before, now brightly danced upon our laps and the crystal absinthia on the cart's silver tray. And of the absinthia, I wasn't surprised that an absinthe service would be part of the suite, the drink being a local mainstay, but I have to say, this particular service was among the finest I'd seen: an ice-filled, crystalline absinthe fountain with a glass fairy at its peak, two crystal reservoir glasses, atop of each, a stainless steel absinthe spoon and a resting rectangular cube of whitened sugar, and beside them, the decanted bottle of the fuchsia colored Providence Six absinthe.

Hansen must've found the service as pleasing; he appeared as eager as I to partake. "May I do the preparations?" he asked.

"That would be splendid," I said.

"Excellent. If you could," he said, nodding toward the floor behind the cart. "The entertainment is in that box right there."

He lifted the decanter of fuchsia absinthe from the cart and held it up and away from us so that we could compare it to the nebula beyond the transparent wall. "I'll be," he said. "The same shade."

"I believe that's the point," I said. "To lead you to believe it's a sample of the actual nebula."

"Brilliant," he said, then slowly drizzled the absinthe over the first sugar cube.

I lifted open the lid of the box. Inside, on a bed of red velvet, were two large chrome hoops—I'd guess they were twenty-five centimeters across, no thicker than a heavy gauge wire—and when I removed them, I found them to be incredibly lightweight. I held them up before me, one in each hand, glimmering in the firelight. "And what are these?" I asked.

"They're headsets," he said.

"Headsets?"

"Yes." Having filled the reservoir of the first glass with absinthe, he moved to pour over the next cube of sugar.

"The penthouse is equipped with a neural lace interface that will allow us to link into a simulation—a virtual world."

"Really?" I said, placing one of the rings upon my head. "They're far more delicate than any neural interfaces I've seen before."

"Well. We're not traveling far."

"No. I suppose not," I said. I puckered my brow. "Where exactly did you have in mind?"

Having finished pouring the absinthe, he slid each of the glasses into place beneath the two fountain taps, then switched them on. Slowly, cold water began to flow from the taps over the cubes and into the reservoirs, transforming the clear fuchsia absinthe to a pink, milky elixir.

He held out a hand. "May I?" he asked.

"Certainly," I said, handing him his ring.

He fit his headset onto his scalp. The reflection of the fire on the chrome created an illusion of illumination and I was curious if mine looked the same. "Well," he said. "We were just speaking of how, as children, we use to play Hide and Seek."

"We're going back to the yards?"

"Dear, no." He shrugged. "Though that may have also been of some satisfaction. But no. With the aid of our neural lace, we're going to play a new game."

"Oh," I said. "I've done the virtual before. But not direct with the lace, just with the suit and goggles."

"Where did you find an old rig like that?"

"There's a place…it's not important. Anyway. I'm intrigued."

With the sugar now melted and the glasses full, Hansen shut off the fountain's taps and the last trickle of ice water ceased to flow. He offered me a glass, took one for himself, then held his up toward the nebula in the same manner as he had with the bottle. I marveled at the small pink cloud as he twisted the small glass in his hand.

"The common name for the nebula," I said, "is the *Eye of God*, and they say—"

He turned to me with a raise of his brow and the curl of a grin. *"They?"*

"Indeed. *They*," I said. *"They* say that the absinthe allows one to peek inside."

"And what say you?"

"I say," I held up my own glass to clink beside his. "I say, cheers to the quest."

"Indeed," he said, clinking his cocktail to mine. "Cheers."

A brutal anise fire of bitter and sweet filled my mouth.

As I swallowed, the liquid lightning burned my throat, sending a warm quiver cascading down my spine then up again, culminating in a slight full body convulsion and an echoing shudder that set my teeth to chatter.

There was a brief calm, then the electric wave pulsed through me again. My stomach responded with a nauseated revulsion, forcing me to gag, but before I could vomit, the sensation ebbed away; in its place, a warmth of euphoria blanketed me.

"Hrrm," said Hansen, clearing his throat. Softly, he added, "That is quite the elixir."

My eyes going wet with tears, I rasped out a, "Quite."

"Cheers," he said again, holding up his glass. I raised mine. With a slight squeak, I responded, "cheers," then finished off the remainder of my glass.

The second drink was far more soothing.

My shoulders grew soft, and my gums numb. I ran my tongue across the back of my teeth and puckered my lips and cheeks. My mouth felt foreign.

I set my absinthe glass back onto the tray, peered to the fire, and instantly winced. My eyes had become suddenly sensitive to the brilliance of the flames. "Whoa," I said softly. I slid deeper into the chair, rested my head back, and let my lids fall closed.

The neural lace linked quickly.

I was no longer sitting in Hansen's library in front of the fire; rather, I was submerged, surrounded by water. My heart jumped and I gasped. *"Relax,"* said Hansen, but not aloud—only in my head. *"You're still breathing."* And I realized I could breathe; or, at least, that I wasn't suffocating.

The threat of drowning passed; I took in my new environment.

I was floating in an endless, inky blue pool that could have as easily been in a large tank or an ocean. Though there were no visible walls or surface, a pale-pink light fought in from high above.

A loud gurgle rushed close behind me, and I spun in time to see a bearded purple merman accelerate past, his tail slamming up and down, leaving a trio of small bubbling cyclones in his wake as he disappeared into the darkness.

"I'll be," I said, and heard my words in my head as I'd heard Hansen's. *"Is that you?"* I asked.

"I don't know who you're referring to," said Hansen. *"But it wasn't me. I'm somewhere else. You'll have to find me."*

"I see," I said.

"Hide and Seek, remember?"

"So I'm 'It'?"

"Actually, in a sort, we both are," he said. *"We have to find each other."*

"Oh. So it's more Seek."

"I suppose. But we're hidden from each other."

"*Do we share clues?*" I asked.

"*Yes,*" he said. "*Exactly. You said you just saw someone. Are you in a public place?*"

"*I'm in the water,*" I said, "*and I just saw a purple merman swim by. I don't know if it's public, the light is dim.*"

"*Quite right.*"

"*You're in the water too?*"

"*No, no. I'm on the surface. No atmosphere. When you gasped, I thought you were too. That's why I reminded you to breathe.*"

"*So how does it work? The game? How do we play?*"

"*We move toward each other,*" he said. "*The first step, I'd guess, is for me to find water or you to find land.*"

"*Providing we're on the same planet.*"

"*I hadn't thought of that. I'm in a small canyon surrounded by a high rock formation.*"

"*Can you see the sky?*" I asked.

"*It's the nebula. Essentially the same view as the window of the penthouse.*"

"*Then we're most likely near each other.*"

"*You see the nebula too?*" he asked.

"*No,*" I said. "*But there's pink light above me. I believe it's coming from the surface.*"

"*I'll try to find higher ground,*" said Hansen. "*Can you swim upward?*"

"*I don't know,*" I said. "*I'll try.*" I swung my arms before me in an attempt to pull myself forward. "*Amazing,*" I said.

"*What is?*"

"*My fingers. They're webbed.*"

"*It's the construct. It will morph your body to fit your environment. Has anything else changed?*"

"*Hold on,*" I said, attempting to right myself. I found that bobbing submerged had a few limitations. For one, when I bent to inspect my feet, I ended up in a somersault, and when I straightened myself back, I flipped the other way. I attempted this a few more times but, though the construct was virtual, fell prey to Newton's third law—for every action I executed, there was an equal and opposite reaction. I spun over so many times that I became dizzy.

Then I decided on a different tact.

Having not succeeded at the many iterations of the maneuver, I waited until I was stabilized then, as gently as I could, simply peeked down past my belly toward my toes.

What I found was a purple scaled, wide finned tail.

Apparently, I was a merman too.

"Amazing," I said again.

"Are your feet webbed too?"

"Something of the sort," I said. *"I think I've figured out what I need to do. And the timing couldn't have be better."*

"Why's that?" Hansen asked.

"I'm not alone down here," I said.

"The merman is back?"

"No. something else."

My visibility was ten meters at best before the inky blue dissipated to black and it was at this shadowy edge of my vision that appeared what at first seemed to be a long, thin line. It ran vertical, an undulating thread, floating closer, taking shape and dimension, until I realized it was not so much a string as the elongated tentacle appendage of something in the darkness beyond.

"What is it?" asked Hansen.

"It's a tentacle," I said. *"Though I'm not quite sure if it's dangling from above or reaching from below."*

"You'd best move away."

My mind was swirling. The nausea returned to my gut. I decided that, unable to see the depths, up was the way out—go for the light and that sort of thing. I placed my arms to my sides, aimed my chin toward the pale-pink, then with the slightest possible effort, moved my toes, or the part of me where toes would be, forward then back then forward again.

The subtle pressure of water pressed onto my face as I moved upward.

"*Okay,*" I said. "*I'm on the move.*"

"*Good. Me too. Let me know when you reach the surface.*"

I pressed forward, or upward as the case may have been. As happens beneath the surface, the pale-pink light stayed the same, never seeming to brighten. I told myself that it would open soon and that, having no reference to this virtual sea, I was simply much deeper than I had thought.

"*Hansen,*" I said after a few minutes in, "*I have to say, this portion of the game is becoming monotonous.*"

"*Don't fret,*" he said. "*You won't have to go too much farther.*"

It was right then that a trail of bubbles rose past me. I watched them as they raced upward, until they faded into the shine of the light.

Then there were more.

I thrashed my tail in an attempt to speed up my ascent. The only sign it was working was that the bubbles' flight slowed.

I bent my head forward. The tentacle was still there, dangling in front of me. Still swimming upward, I let my eyes dart to my peripheral, to the right, to the left. What I found was that the incidents of tentacle had multiplied. In fact, I was surrounded by undulating tentacle strands.

More bubbles rushed past, and I dared to peek down, into the darkness below.

There, barely lit, gently rising beneath me, was the form of a beast.

My heart raced. I kicked franticly, slamming my tail back and forth, in an effort to get away. But it was hopeless. The creature was too large and overtook me as easily as floating upward.

Its tentacles drew close to me and I stopped pushing upward or risked ensnaring myself in its grasp.

"Hansen," I softly said, *"I don't like this game anymore."*

"Hmm," he said. *"I have a confession."*

"You don't like it either?"

"I've never liked it. But I thought it was fitting."

"Fitting? But how?"

"It was the game we played as children."

"I want to stop now." I placed my hands to my head but found no chromium band. *"How do we stop?"*

"You can't," he said.

"What do you mean we can't stop?"

"That's part of the confession. I had Alena add something to the absinthe. A bit of a lock, if you will."

"A lock?"

"The Providence Six Absinthe is a strong distraction, but not strong enough for my intent. I needed to be sure I could anesthetize your body but still have access to your mind."

"Hansen? Why would you do such a thing?"

"Ah, you see, Conrad, that's the other part of the confession. I'm not Hansen."

"Well then. Who are you?" I asked.

"Would you believe, Benny Melker?"

"I don't understand. Melker?"

"Yes. You see the story about driving Hansen to succeed is true. He tracked me down—to rub my face in it, I suppose. Thing is, I was quite happy to see him. When he found me, I was in a bit of financial peril, and he was a convenient remedy to my ills. Hansen

may have been successful in status and station, but he was still weak and easily manipulated. I tricked him into a virtual game of Hide and Seek, then trapped him in the game in order to take possession of his body and fortune."

"That's criminal," I said. "You evolved from a bully to a full-blown criminal."

"Matter of perspective, I guess. You see, from mine, I was the one who was bullied by the rest of the class. Treated as a gnat. Your words, not mine, but equivalent. Now, it was never my intention to be vindictive, to seek revenge. It wasn't until Hansen showed up to gloat that the opportunity presented itself. It was spontaneous, but I have to say that it worked so well, I've repeated the task several times."

"Repeated?" I asked. The tentacles that a moment before had been floating around me began to settle on my flesh, wrapping around me as they did. Tightening.

"With Hansen's fortune, I had a sudden influx of capital, a financial means and, like you, all the time in the world. So I hunted down all of the old classmates, one by one. Attaining their fortunes. Joston, Martin, Riley—each and every one. And Conrad, I plan to do the same to you."

I found myself engulfed, the thin tentacles coiled around me, squeezing. With barely a breath, I exclaimed, "Melker, you're a monster!"

"Ha, ha, ha," laughed Melker. "Conrad, I have another confession. I'm not on the surface. I'm right here with you."

ABOUT THE AUTHORS

Gustavo Bondoni is an Argentine writer with over a hundred stories published in fourteen countries, in seven languages, and is a winner in the **National Space Society's "Return to Luna" Contest** and the **Marooned Award for Flash Fiction** (2008). His fiction has appeared in the **Texas STAAR English Test cycle, The Rose & Thorn, Albedo One, The Best of Every Day Fiction** and many others.

His latest books are a comic fantasy romp: **The Malakiad** (2018) and a military SF adventure, **Incursion** (2017). He has also published two science fiction novels: **Outside** (2017) and **Siege** (2016). He has also recently published an ebook novella entitled **Branch**. His previously published short fiction is collected in **Tenth Orbit and Other Faraway Places** (2010) and **Virtuoso and Other Stories** (2011). **The Curse of El Bastardo** (2010) is a short fantasy novel.

For news and updates visit gustavobondoni.com

M. M. De Voe writes interstitial fiction and has been published in magazines ranging from the **St. Petersburg Review** to **Daily Science Fiction**. Her poetry has won first place in the **Lyric** as well as the **NYC's PoetTweet** contest. She has also won top prizes in flash fiction, literary fiction and horror, and co-wrote a sci-fi musical that was produced by Tisch School of the Arts. Founder of the literary nonprofit **Pen Parentis**, she lives in Manhattan, writes what she likes, and does the next thing on a daily basis.

For news and updates visit mmdevoe.com

Ann Stolinsky is the founder and owner of Gontza Games, an independent board and card game company. Several of her stories have been published in the last few years.

Jessica West (a.k.a. West1Jess) is currently pursuing a state of self-induced psychosis, also known as writing. In the past, she has worked for Wal-Mart, a lawyer, and a bank. Now if she could just get a couple years experience with the IRS and the NSA, world domination is in the bag.

Jess lives in Acadiana with three daughters still young enough to think she's cool and a husband who knows better but likes her anyway.

For news and updates visit west1jess.com

Daniel Arthur Smith is a USA Today bestselling author. His titles include *Spectral Shift*, *Hugh Howey Lives*, *The Cathari Treasure, The Somali Deception*, and a few other novels and short stories. He also curates the phenomenal short fiction series *Tales from the Canyons of the Damned* and *Frontiers of Speculative Fiction*.

He was raised in Michigan and graduated from Western Michigan University where he studied philosophy, with focus on cognitive science, meta-physics, and comparative religion. He began his career as a bartender, barista, poetry house proprietor, teacher, and then became a technologist and futurist for the Fortune 100 across the Americas and Europe.

Daniel has traveled to over 300 cities in 22 countries, residing in Los Angeles, Kalamazoo, Prague, Crete, and now writes in Manhattan where he lives with his wife and young sons.

For news and updates visit danielarthursmith.com